Looking
Through
the
Wood Knot Hole

Copyright Information

Copyright © 2023 by Anna Schoenbach

First Printing: April, 2020

Second Printing: January, 2021

Third Printing: March, 2023

ISBN: 9798592905568

ASIN: B087Y6WLFB

Imprint: Independently published

This book is dedicated to Rock Creek Park, Skyland Drive in Shenandoah National Park, and to all who appreciate the beauty and ferocity of nature.

Introduction

The first story you learned was probably a story about animals doing something very foolish or something very clever. You likely first heard the story as a child, but you probably remember its lesson to this day. That is the power of fables.

Fables have been used for thousands of years to teach lessons. Whether these stories were told to children, adults, or anyone in between, the antics of wolves, foxes, ravens, grasshoppers, and ants, have taught people right from wrong. Through these animal avatars of humanities' flaws, fables have helped generations of humans to thrive in this world and to be good neighbors to each other. We learned from them in the past and we still have much to learn from them today.

The original fables and fairy tales were very grim and harsh, and my poems follow suit. Animals suffer and die, and those that survive must learn from their mistakes or fail to survive for much longer.

In my short poems and parables, these animals are reflections of humanity, but I try to keep the details factual – a residual habit from my day job as a freelance science and medical writer. However, in these poems and their creatures, the facts also hold a deeper meaning:

- Be happy with what you have, and anything more is pleasant but extra.

- Many things change with time, sometimes for the better.

- Care can preserve but anxiety can destroy.

- Good things come to those who wait, but only when the groundwork has already been done.

- The world is much harsher for the selfish.

The rest is for you to interpret from the 31 poems that I, with the humbleness of the forest beasts that speak within them, present to you in this collection.

When I first started writing these poems in 2018, I was in the middle of tempering my expectations and holding back my ego. I was growing up, facing a harsh, dark world that was not the world that I expected and, at times, not the world that I wanted to be in. It is now 2021, and I am still learning to endure the sometimes-cruel whimsy of reality.

These poems helped me to survive and continue to add joy and meaning to my life. I think it will do the same for you, too.

Enjoy. Learn. Grow.

TABLE OF CONTENTS

The Caterpillar and the Grasshopper

The caterpillar and the grasshopper were not friends.

"You are fat" said the grasshopper.

"You are ugly".

The caterpillar took the abuse and kept eating

because they knew they must eat.

The grasshopper came every day

to bother the caterpillar, as they grew and grew

on the leaves of the mulberry tree.

"You smell" they said.

"You look like bird poop."

The caterpillar remained silent,

as a shadow passed over head.

Quick as the wind,

the grasshopper was swept away,

crushed in the beak of a bird.

The caterpillar was not one to be spiteful

but the temptation was too great.

"I may look like it myself," they said,

to the now-empty branch,

"but now you *are* bird poop."

The caterpillar then found a comfortable
branch

and spun its silk cocoon

and emerged, weeks later,

as an elegant, satin-white moth,

with only a few days to live.

Living Under a Rock

The worm was not a bad creature
though slimy, squirmy, and low-born,
they ate the dirt and detritus
that no one wanted
and refreshed the soil they passed through
but still, they were not liked.

The owl took offense to the worm's
blindness,
the cat, to its slimy-smooth skin,
the robin only wished to eat it,
and the beetle simply did not care
if the worm lived or died.

The worm was hurt by their barbs
and sought to do well by them all.
"If I stay under this rock"
said the worm,
"then I will offend no one."

And the worm stayed there, inoffensively,

in the dark and moistened cold.

The owl still felt that the worm was absurd,

the cat still complained,

the robin lamented that the worm was, now, hidden,

and the beetle still didn't care.

Despite this, it wasn't so bad under the rock.

The worm lived there

alone.

The worm died there

alone.

And there is not much more to say than that.

The Fox and the Empty Hole

The fox sat,

staring at a burrow

so patiently that the indifferent crow

had to come over to ask,

"Why do you sit and stare at a hole,

"when nothing is happening,

"or has happened,

"for several hours?"

"I am waiting" said the fox.

"There is a rat in this burrow. It is small and delicious."

"Why not dig for it?" asked the crow,

it's talons were not suited for digging

and rat was not on its menu.

"If I wait here, it will come to me," said the fox,

"it will leap into my paws, and I will eat it."

The crow watched from a tree,

eating nuts and scraps from roadkill.

He watched the fox

wait,

and wait,

for days.

The fox shivered in the snow

and starved.

The crow supposed he could have fed the fox

with his nuts,

and with his scraps from roadkill,

or with the berries that grew nearby,

but someone who wouldn't work for their food

wasn't worth a caw.

The Once Alpha[1]

The wolf led his pack
together they hunted
together they fed
together they brooded and howled.

There was a problem in the pack,
one member
who worked well with the others
but not with him.

He knew a challenge would come in due time,
so he harassed and he snapped,
pushing the interloper away,
halting his claim, at every step, at every hunt,
at every feeding.

And in time, the leader became less efficient,
and the hunts became less successful,
the food less plentiful,
the pack less under his control.

Then they turned on their leader

tearing out his fur and his authority

with growls and snarls.

They sent him running, tail between his
legs.

When he returned he was no one,

shamed for the rest of his days,

led by his challenger

to live in constant fear.

The pack reached new success,

howling the loudest in the wilds.

They had many new litters and pups.

They prospered.

And the once-alpha,

was now omega,

scorned, hungry

succumbing to his folly.

Acorns and Labor

A squirrel decided to work extra hard this
year
gathering acorns
burying them in caches in strange places
to feed him in the long, cold months.

Every acorn in the forest was taken,
buried, stored away.
But, when winter came, the squirrel kept
working.
He had to have all of the nuts he could find!
He buried them throughout the forest
stored away for the snowy days
that kept ever coming.

Like the snow, he was tireless.
The other squirrels admired his efforts,
while they fed off his stored nuts
and grew fat off his labor,
as he worked blindly for himself.

When spring came,

there was a new forest of young oaks

reaching for the fresh sunlight,

and many fat forest animals

praising the squirrel who sustained them,

Who was now quite cold,

quite thin,

and long dead.

The Bat's Freedom

Every evening, the bat leaves her pup in the cave

to fly out in the open sky.

Her pup envies this

but he cannot follow her.

He must wait for her to return

huddled with his fellow pups.

And he was sick of it.

The outside world must be a wonderful place

full of fresh air and wind.

He wanted to see a place not crowded with bats.

"I want to go" he said to his neighbors,

"I want to fly in the open sky."

His friends told him to follow his dreams

and fly.

"Then I will."
Proudly, he unhooked
his thumbs from the cave ceiling
and tried to flap his undeveloped wings
and, like all fools with dreams,

fell.

The Owl and the Sunrise

What was behind the bar-feathered owl?

It could be a predator, he worried.

He turned his entire head a full circle around

to peer into the shadows at his tail.

He gazed, fearfully, for many minutes

and he thought he saw movement,

fleeting through the trees,

his wings primed for a fast escape.

Instead, all he saw was shadows, moving and wakening

and the end of his hunting time, revealing

both his fear and his folly

and giving him no more than a pain in his neck.

As he faced behind him,

looking for a threat - only leaves on the
trees -

the owl missed the spectacle in front of him:

a sunrise gleaming with the promise of day.

Like Eggshells

Sparrows chatter, chirping, flapping to and fro,

like many, they are angry

at the changes in the world.

"Today's nestlings," one railed, "are delicate and soft."

"Yes, yes, soft like down, delicate like eggshells," said another,

"say the wrong word for the wrong thing

"and

"they

"crack."

"I weep for the new generation, too weak willed to fly

"against the blustering wind,

"how will such sensitive souls fare

"in the winter to come?"

The new generation of sparrows hopped and fed

and ignored their elders,

knowing that the future was theirs,

and that one day they would be the ones complaining

on their perches in the sun.

The hawk, roosting in the branches overhead,

listened to their ramblings

and to some extent,

they agreed!

At times, it seemed,

the ire of these young little birds was stoked

at the most innocent of phrases and gestures,

and the hawk did not always understand.

"But," he thought, gazing sharp-eyed

into the understory growth teeming with small feathered shapes,

young and old,

"though differences of ideas may split this flock apart,

"in the end they are the same,

"from sparrow to crow;"

"All who are foolish enough to fly

"when I am in the sky

"are my prey,

"'eggshells' or no."

The Cardinal

The little cardinal was brown and drab.

Though the color helped him hide, he was frustrated

for red was his favorite color.

Though he was already several months old,

he was not yet an adult, not yet grown enough for red.

He wondered when he would get his red feathers.

"When it's time" said his mother.

"Not too soon" said his father.

The little cardinal did not understand

that neither wished him to grow up.

His mother, because she enjoyed

his peeping cries

his fluttering wings

the feeding, beak to beak.

His father, because other males were competition

and when he was red at last

he would be a threat

and he did not wish

to combat his son,

not yet.

But the little cardinal thought his father was beautiful.

He wanted to be an adult

like his father,

to sing

like his father,

to take wing

like his father.

To be red like his father - this, he could change:

He found a pail sitting beside a house, and,

When his mother's back was turned,

the little bird

dipped

into the thick color within.

His feathers became ruddy and perfect.

For a moment, he tasted adulthood and
loved it.

Then the paint weighed him down

and he fluttered, struggling to be free.

And his parents watched

helpless,

anguished,

as he tried not to drown

in his newfound maturity.

The Ambition of Ants

The ants wished to carve a masterpiece,

a nest to be the king of all nests,

a garden, a nursery, a queen chamber,

that all other ants

would declare to be the best.

Together they worked in perfect unison,

digging and working the earth

into the grandest corridors, the largest
chambers,

vast halls and galleries

to rival the gods.

The queen bred her workers,

drones swarmed around her,

workers dug deep,

and then all of them died

when the endless carving

was too much for the earth

and the grand castle -

the envy of all ants -

became a mere sinkhole

littered with writhing larvae.

Easy pickings for other, lower beasts.

Of Wood and Wood-Eaters

"I cannot stand
"to work with you
"so foul, so disgusting,
I hate you!"
the termite said, to the bacteria
hiding in its stomach.

"This is true, this is true,"
the bacteria agreed
in unison, as a film
in the termite's gut."
"That we are disgusting to you,
"we do agree,
"but necessary to your feast,
upon this tree."

"I cannot stand to work with you,"
the termite snarled,
"cannot stand it at all,
"and so, I won't."

And he vomited up all the bacteria in his stomach

and starved

because he could no longer digest

the wood he so loved to chew.

And the bacteria returned.

"That we were disgusting to you,

"we do agree,

"but if you would not work with us,

" you could not eat your tree,

"and now, instead,

"we will feast on *thee*."

And the bacteria did not starve.

Sacrifice

The bee, a male, knew his purpose.

He saw his fellow drones swarming around
a new queen,

dying in blazes of pleasure

as they passed on their seed and

then fell.

He didn't want to die

and so, hung back until she retreated.

He died anyway in the Fall

when his sisters kicked him out

into the crisping cold.

The other drone's sired offspring,

offspring who would become queens,

and workers who would keep the colony
alive,

and drones who would continue the
species.

But this male bee died,

Purposeless and lost,

Coated by the first frost,

all alone.

Up a Waterfall

"It's been 3 years," the salmon said,

"will our spawning ground look as it did

3 years before?"

"We won't know," said his friend,

"until we see it, and, I hope

"to see it with you."

The salmon changed,

as he moved from ocean to stream,

face hooked, skin colored, gills adapted to
water without salt.

He knew waves, but soon he saw before
him

a waterfall, a wall of water, so tall, so
ferocious.

He hesitated.

"You can do it," said his friend, her eyes
bright

as she looked

to the top of the falls.

"Merely swim, merely try,

"and try and try and fail and try again."

So he tried.

He fought against gravity,

fought against the ravaging water pounding
against his scales,

fought up the falls only to slip back down to
the pool at the bottom.

"Don't worry!" said his friend, "Try again,

"and surely, eventually, you will succeed."

He watched as she leapt the falls

and into a bear's waiting grasp,

and he tried again, fighting the water,

and found himself slipping into the current

and against sharp rocks

that lined the fall's edge.

Briefly he glimpsed her torn form, the bear's
meal,

as the light left her eyes and her roe spilled
from her belly,

and he knew that,

while failure was not always failure,

success was not always success.

"You were right," he said, thanking her

as he continued his journey and swam

to the next waterfall to try again.

The Catch

The waterfall,

the station of the bear,

where he waits for flopping bodies to leap

over the cresting water.

Claws ready, mouth ready,

the bear tenses,

senses,

strikes,

and, in a grasping claw holds a fat salmon!

"This salmon will feed me well this winter."

"I shall eat it whole,

"strip flesh and fat from bone."

"So proud am I,

"for with my skill, I caught it on my first
swipe."

But the bear gloated over the fish

a moment too long,

and the fish found its way
out of the bear's grasping claws,
escaping the cage of its sharp jaws,
back to the waters not far below.

The bear's first catch
proved to be beginner's luck,
for fish after fish evaded his grasp.
By the end of the salmon run
he had nothing to show for his pride.

Eternity

The tree thought it would live forever,
strong of leaf and bough,
but then the xylem arteries of its trunk
clogged
and it choked and died away.

The termites
chewing away at the tree's dead wood
thought their meal would last forever,
but a woodpecker came,
pecked them from their tunnels,
and made them her meal instead.

The fungus that grew on the rotted wood
thought that it's home would last forever,
under its fungal strands,
but a fire came and scorched them bare -
and only ash remained.

When an owl came

and saw the battered and hollowed tree,

with its scars of rot, and searing, and beak-
holes.

It knew that it's nest would not last forever.

One day, it's new shelter would fall.

One day, it would be no more.

But, for as long as the dead tree lasted,

as long as the owl lived in it,

it would be home.

The Moth and the Cicada

The moth and the cicada rested on a moonlit branch.

"I do hope we find mates," said the cicada mournfully,

for his song, yet again, brought no females to lay his eggs.

"We will!" Said the moth, his antennae full of the scent of hope,

for he could smell the females in their homes,

could sense where they laired,

and he knew that he would find them one day.

"So - let us not despair!"

The cicada accepted his wisdom,

the wisdom of many nights.

His mates would come, if he kept singing,

high up in his trees.

"Moth, my friend, who is your true and ideal mate?" the cicada asked.

The moth laughed,"Why, a moth of perfectly round body,

"wings cloud white, her antennae a perfect shape,

"her scent the perfect blend

"of crisp and warmth.

"I'll tell you, my friend,"

the moth paused,

"I should like to mate with the moon."

"But the moon is too far!" the cicada proclaimed,

"no matter how far you fly,

"you will never reach her!"

The moth only laughed.

"But see, my friend," the moth said, "if I try, there is a chance…

"and a chance is a chance,

"and so worth the try!"

He fluttered in the confidence of his wings.

"But what of you, my friend?

"Who is your ideal mate?"

"If she comes to me, and sings with me,"

the cicada trilled,

"then she is my perfect mate,

"the one I waited forty years for,

"sipping sap deep in the dirt."

"With standards like that,"

the moth laughed, though not mockingly,

"you will be sure to find your mate."

And it turns out both were true.

For the moth tried to court the moon

and flew to her, to mate with her,

only to find that she was a porch lamp,

and burn to his death.

And the cicada sang his longing, sang his grief,

sang of his wayward friend, and his loneliness on the branch.

And, remembering his friend's words, kept

singing.

And later in the season, there came another,

and she sang a duet with him.

From high upon his branch,

their eggs fell to the soil below,

to wait out many winters,

as they too perished in the last brilliant rays of summer,

clasped in each other's claws.

Of Trash and Trouble

Two glowing eyes met on a moonlit night.

A cat and a racoon shared hot stares

over a piece of trash.

"It's mine, I saw it first."

The racoon reached for its prize.

"It is in my territory," explained the cat,

"and though I do not want this trash,

"and though it will cause my fur to reek,

"I, on principle, cannot let you take it."

"It is mine, and I will take it."

And so, the cat's claws came out.

Though there were many pieces of trash
around,

even a few steps away, beyond the cat's
scented realm,

the racoon was also a beast of principle,

and they did battle, screaming, into the
night.

By morning, both were tired,

bruised and bloodied,

and the racoon limped away

prize less.

The cat limped away victorious,

but found that a rival

had marked his favorite spot as his own

and, so adamant about the racoon and his trash,

he had not been there to defend it.

All in all, a loss.

The Deer's Choice

A young bird came upon a deer

lying in a bed of flowers.

"Why are you here?

said the bird,

"The human will not come out to bring us
seeds

"if, lazily, you lie there,"

The deer looked up,

"Forgive me, little bird,"

he said with a tired tone,

"but I can do no more than lie,

"and die,

"though I'm glad not to die alone."

He lifted his forepaw,

and the little bird could see

that he was muddied,

gravely injured, and bloodied.

The bird hopped, it's quick feet anxious,

"But can't you move, just for a bit?"

"No", the deer shook his un-antlered head.

"My leg is broken, my hindquarters bloodied,

"my blood burns in my veins and I ache.

"I have walked far to be here, and I can walk no longer,

"and soon I will be dead."

The bird chirped "Can't you move just a little? Over there? Away?"

"If the human does not bring your seeds,"

said the deer,

"it is not my fault.

"I am sorry for your need,

"but you will have to feed elsewhere,

"because I cannot leave."

"Cannot, or will not?"

The little bird was irate,

"Seems to me you could hobble away,

"and die somewhere else."

The deer looked at his flowers,

and laid down his weary head.

"No. I may not have chosen when or how to die,

"but I will choose where I die,

"here in this bed of sweet flowers and grass,

"in the warm sun, near the cool shade of this stone wall,

"protected from all further ravages."

"So," said the deer, "here I will die."

In her indignance, the little bird shrieked.

She stabbed at him with her tiny claws, her anger peaked.

She hit him with her small wings.

She hopped upon his body long after he had stopped breathing,

his fur barely ruffled

in the warm spring sun.

She did not starve, her flock ensured it,

and eventually her seeds did arrive some hours later.

But a hawk would come for the little bird one day

and as she bled, pierced by its talons,

she would remember the deer

and envy its peaceful death on his bed of flowers.

Sweetened Labor Shared

Bees buzz in springtime verdant.

Two share a flower, with enough bounty for both

but only just.

"Sister, I am gladdened by your company," spoke a worker

for it was hard work to drink nectar from a flower,

and long going in the bright sun,

and the bee was not cut out for lonely work.

"As am I, for both your company and your industry

"as well."

"What a bounteous day and a beautiful sky."

"Indeed, a day that will be productive,

"as we bring this nectar to the hive."

"Even now, our sisters beat their wings

"to dry what we have collected before."

"The honey that will scent the hive

"is our reward."

"Days of labor, for such a beautiful thing!"

"Our gold," agreed the workers.

Their bellies full, they alighted,

following the map that the sun traced in the sky.

Over the course of their lives, they had gathered

many body weights of nectar,

only enough for a mere drop of honey,

but enough to fill a belly or two;

two bellies

that would not starve in the cold months.

But returning, the sisters found

their hive in ruins,

their kin buzzing in a stinging cloud

about a bear, honey coated,

swiping lazily at the bees.

"What have you done?!" the sisters cried,

"Why have you done this?"

The lazy bear sighed,

months of labor dripping wastefully from his snout.

"I was hungry," he said, swiping his paw.

They stung it, and thus ended their lives.

Their stings did not penetrate the bear's thick hide.

He wandered away

so that he could survive the cold months

on the fat

of another's hard sweet work.

Settled

Eight eggs laid, eight eggs beneath,

warming in her downy nest.

In the long days waiting for her mate,

the goose entertains herself.

The goose counts her eggs again,

eight eggs, always eight.

Today a round stone appeared,

round and speckled like an egg.

The goose, alone, panics.

Has she missed an egg? Was one lost?

The goose counts her eggs again,

eight eggs. Always eight.

Still, she stares at it, it worries her.

She knows better, it is not hers.

The goose counts her eggs again,

eight eggs. Always eight.

But she cannot look away. She cannot stop thinking,

about the little round stone.

Finally, she can ignore it no more.

She waddles out and nudges it side to side

before tucking it beneath her beak,

and rolls it - oh so carefully -

back to her nest,

where she places it tidily among her eggs.

The goose settles onto her nest once more,

downy body touching downy nest,

warming her sleeping goslings in their
shells.

Relieved, the goose counts her eggs again.

Nine eggs.

Always nine.

The Dog's Honest Truth

The world was not always kind to the dog
and the dog accepted that this was so.
But he wanted to be loved,
liked,
acknowledged,
and so he had an idea.

There was a key to being liked
the dog had realized,
and that was being likable,
so he laughed, he barked
and wagged his tail
and offered his honest love to all.

But he was scorned,
for he was "annoying,"
his barking too loud,
his love unwelcomed.

They hit him,

called him dirty,

laughing at his prancing.

Still, joy was infectious.

When old age came to claim him,

though the dog died alone,

he died happy

because, though others might not like him,

he at least liked himself.

Across the Water

The lizard and the mouse waited

by the river, calm.

Both could swim very well

but even here these friends agreed

the water was too deep,

too wide,

for either to cross on their own.

"We'll wait and see," said the lizard, calm.

"Someone may come who we can ask for
help."

"We cannot wait!" whispered the fearful
mouse.

"No one will come! Or, they will come too
late! Or, they may eat us!"

"We will be fine," the lizard reassured his
nervous friend.

"If need be, we can flee, and merely lose a
tail."

The mouse, who had escaped tooth and
claw before,

and had only one tail to lose,

went silent.

But even he knew that to go with the lizard

was better than being alone.

Getting to the other side was worth it,

so he snuggled close to his friend's scaly
hide to wait.

An otter, lithe and smooth, came dancing
down the bank.

The mouse shuddered at its sharp claws

and the sharp teeth in its grinning mouth

and urged his friend to wait.

(If they had to hitch a ride, at least let it be
an herbivore!)

But the lizard ignored the warnings and
stepped forward.

"Excuse me," said the lizard,

"my friend and I must cross, but it is too far
to swim,

"so if it would not be too much trouble

"could you take us, please, to the other side?"

The otter looked down on the tiny things.

"No trouble at all," she said,

"hop on my back and hold on

"it will not take too long."

The lizard leapt aboard,

grasping with his flexible paws.

The mouse followed,

and together with his friend,

hoped to survive

to see the other side.

So it was the mouse's turn to be brave.

"Thank you so much," said the mouse,

wary as his kind were wont,

"for we go across to lair with our kin

"to gather food to survive the long Winter in plenty and in warmth."

Danger, his mother always taught,

was best diffused with sweetness.

"Have you, good otter, family you need to feed?

"For winter is hard on all of us, and we should compensate you,

"for your trouble and lost time!"

"It is no trouble," the otter said,

making good time, mid-stream now,

"I have no family and no clan,

"so my fishing is for myself alone,

"and my lair is lonely, but snug."

"You are welcome to join us." said the lizard,

"When chill of winter comes,

"all are welcome to take refuge from its bitter cold.

"Uniting against it, all survive, to resume our struggles in Spring."

The otter sighed - "Oh how nice it must be,

"to share the winter with family and friends,

"but living alone is much less work!"

They passed the midway mark, in the midst of the shimmering water, and the otter laughed, sudden and loud.

"No," she added, "indeed, I'd better not,

"for our preparations are, it seems, not a match,

"but I thank you all the same."

She stopped at the other edge and lowered her head

to let the two small creatures off.

"Thank you!"

said the mouse relieved, as he disembarked.

"Yes, thank you," said the lizard,

"for we would not have been able to cross,

"without your generous help."

"You are very welcome," the otter said, "but you see,

"you almost did not."

"For I intended," she reared up grinning, her teeth sharp, "to drown you,

"and then eat you in the water while you squirmed,

"but you were both so polite, so kind and generous in my grasp,

"I could not bring myself to do it.

"So, I wish you luck in the winter, and, too,

"that you keep the good hearts

"you saved yourselves with today."

And with a cackle, the otter splashed into
the water behind her

swimming to resume her own hunt

leaving her frightened passengers

to scurry off to the shore beyond

where their family and friends waited

in fur-lined hollows

warm and safe below ground.

Its Love

The cuckoo chick killed its nestmates.

Now it was only its parent-slaves and itself
in the nest,

a parasite upon their own good will.

Its true mother checked in, and saw that
this was

as it should be

for a member of cuckoo-kind.

But in the end, she was wrong.

For the cuckoo learned from its parent-
slaves

who soon became more parent than slave

and where the chick became more host
than parasite.

Though its body was that of a cuckoo,

its mind was as much their child

as its slain nest-siblings.

And so, when it left the nest,

it left as *their* child,

with love unconditional.

And so,

when the time came to leave its own nestling

in a foreign nest, to be a parasite,

and to curse the nest of another bird,

it remembered its parents,

and spared them.

Corvids in Contempt

Two blue jays mock the others, take their
seeds by force.

The beautiful bullies feast alone, jeering, in
the clearing,

as others watch.

They taunt their cousin, the crow, for his dull
coat of black,

because their shimmering feathers are like
the sky.

The sparrow feels the brunt of their
contempt

as only one of many little speckled brown
birds.

So unremarkable! So boring!

The jays laugh at the cardinal and the
canary,

for colorful though they be, like the little
sparrow,

they are small and easily pushed away.

The mourning doves are stupid and drab.

The robin, red-breasted, are cowards for

their annual flight!

The woodpecker, they taunt, pecking at trees all day,

eating grubs, not seeds, like any sane bird.

The woodpecker sees them first,

then the sparrows,

then the cardinal, the robin,

and then the others.

Watching the skies, they all fall silent,

as the falcon and his mate dive down for the kill.

Shrieks followed bloody talons

and, when only fluttering blue feathers remained,

the crow began to crow.

The Coward's Prize

The garbage pile was a feast for the flea-
bitten coyote.

She gorged on rotten meat and spoiled
bananas

as she waded through the colorful ooze to
seize her prize.

In this city, rats knew not to fear her jaws,

for why should she work for fresh meat

when humans throw out so much?

Her ears pricked at the shout of a human,

and knew she was in their territory,

so she grabbed what she could get

and ran away.

It smelled as ripe and rich as the rest,

a most delicious catch, but then realized too
late

that it was just an old cloth, stained and
inedible,

a coward's catch.

But the coyote was not concerned.

There would always be another scent on the wind,

another lazy catch,

another rotten feast.

For now, a drink of filthy rain water

will see her through.

Survive and Thrive

Beneath the soil, tasty things sleep:

this the boar knew.

Snuffling at the ground, he found,

mushrooms plump and flavorful.

Up in the boughs, tasty things sleep:

this the serpent knew.

In the trees, he sees,

neatly wrapped eggs, their richness hidden
in twigs.

Behind thorns, tasty things sleep:

this the bear knew.

Be they stingers or spines, he would find

the sweet berries and honey they guard.

Patience procures what seeking endures.

Boar, serpent, and bear survive.

All indulge innocently and, doing so,

guiltlessly and happily, thrive.

Where She Was Safe

The hare pauses, her haunches tense,

she was still as stone, her every sense

like her fur bristling in the meadow.

With every beam of light, every sultry
shadow,

she felt pinned by sharp and slitted eyes.

Every twig, each wind-swept sigh,

was a carnivore, sharp of teeth,

waiting to take her and crush her beneath.

The grass no longer seemed so green.

Fear quivered in her chest, nothing seen.

But still too much, so she fled,

bolting to her burrow, hidden, instead.

Safe in cool darkness, she relaxed,

spent from her run, her vigil, laxed,

Only to be pierced by sharp fangs –

She screams, stares past the roots that
hang

to the serpent lurking in her home.

And she knew, had she continued to roam

in the light, in the open space,

she would have been, possibly, safe.

Bright Yellow Envy

The canary was jealous of the flowers'
bright plumage

so it plucked away at it, petal by petal, until
only the stamen remained.

"Ha," he said to the flower, now bare,

"now I am the brightest of us, on land or in
air,

"I cannot be beat and you –

"can no longer challenge my splendor."

"Ah," said the flower,

"but do you not see,

"the winter is coming, and now

"no bee or beast will see me

"and come to seed me.

"And I will produce no seed."

"Why gloat about that?" chirped the bird

perched inquisitive on the flower's stem.

"Instead, it seems to me,

"that I have won!"

He puffed his chest out proudly,

"In more ways than one!"

"This is true," said the flower,

"you have hurt me greatly, but you have hurt yourself far more,

"because you have prevented my seed,

"and you now cannot feed from me

"and in the cold months,

"you will go hungry."

"I do not need your seeds," laughed the bird.

"There are other flowers, other seeds, and many ways to feed."

With that, he flew away, bright in the sky,

but it did not take long before he found another flower,

and another, and another,

all brighter than he.

He plucked them bare,

too angered by their petals to prepare

and winter took him unaware.

Bigger birds took the seeds, hardier birds
took the bright berries,

and scurrying beasts buried the rest

beneath the ice and snow.

The little canary retreated to the gardens,

and there he found only barren flowers,

their little dry twigs, snow-killed,

holding no more seeds for his future –

only seeds already buried

and sleeping in the ground to wake up for
the next spring.

The canary scrounged and starved,

froze and cried,

and finally died.

Its bright yellow feathers,

the brightest of all on land or sky,

dampened only so slightly,

drifting away in the snow.

Lessons of the Strays

Old cat, young cat,

no blood between them.

The elder could not move,

the younger groomed his fur.

The elder thirsted desperately

as his body failed

so the younger helped him to water.

The elder was blind,

the younger brought him fish.

"Let me tell you a story," the old cat said.

The young cat listened, rapt,

because the older cat's paws had taken him
far --

from a sodden plastic bag,

a tiny form rescued on the edge of a road.

Old cat long dead,

young cat now older, wiser.

Wild, yet sleek and glossy,

the cat sought to pass on the favor

to a puppy in a rain-soaked box –

his new student, mottled and alone.

"Let me tell you a story," the cat said.

For a time, the puppy hung onto his words,

until one day he did not.

"Why should I listen?" said the now - dog,
"Why should I care?

"Your stories are not mine."

"Because," said the cat, "one day you will
pass this on,

"and another lonely castaway will be saved
by hand or paw."

The dog laughed at the cat, "There is no
point to that."

With the lessons of the strays,

the dog and cat survived, thrived,

in their harsh world.

The cat hoped the dog would come around,

for he cared for them deeply,

but the dog's loyalty went only as far as the
cat

and even then, when his rakish grin
charmed humans

and they took him into their warm, safe,
hands,

the cat was abandoned for luxury.

The dog lived a long and full life,

but died alone, quietly,

in a room that smelled of death and
chemicals.

The humans he had charmed

could not bear to see him die,

so they left him alone.

And the cat?

He again lived the life of his mentor.

Another student, another lost soul -

a bird this time, fallen from its nest, lost to
its family.

The cat aged swiftly in the rain and sun,

but the bird stayed by his side.

Grooming his tired form with its beak,

feeding him scraps piece by piece,

listening to his stories.

The cat's death came slowly as his body
failed,

a cruel specter in the night

but he was not alone, loved at the end.

The bird, his companion,

pledged to carry on the tradition

of lessons for companionship.

One day, the bird would find her own stray,

her own student, lost in the world.

One day, she would say,

"Let me tell you a story."

And none of them would be forgotten.

Amid the Memory of Hooves

Once there had been many hooves – down
this path they trod!

Today, there were only four.

A massive moose grunted, shaking his vast
antlers,

as he remembered times gone by,

when this place echoed with those many
hooves,

and many who had gone away still walked,-

warm by his side.

The massive moose followed the old paths.

Paths once trod by many hooves,

his own, more than once, in the company of
others,

and now, more than once, alone.

Each prong on his vast rack,

seemed to commemorate one more herd-
mate lost

to cold, to fang, to bullet,

to accident in the hungry wood,

to age as unrelenting as any hunting wolf.

They were lost but then replaced by new calves,

but they were not the same, not the same,

but enough to redeem the old.

The moose let out a bellow for old times' sake.

He heard no response.

The moose would find a mate in Fall

but he could not let that distract him now.

The memory of many hoofbeats of the family

he once had, now lost,

could well lead him astray.

Lost in his memories, he stumbled

into traps and sinkholes deep in the snow.

Old times could be dangerous.

He escaped this year.

Next year could take him too.

He bellowed again

and heard an answering call,

another lonely soul.

Though distant, he let them keep him
company

with his memories

in the dead-silent winter night.

Coexistence

The bobcat mother had always been told

"Avoid humans at all costs,

"for they are the most capricious of beasts."

But she and her kits needed a warm, safe place to sleep.

She strode to them with confidence,

because, she had learned, all creatures respond to confidence.

If you pretend that you belong there, if you act like you believe it,

then others will believe it too.

She sniffed the clear wall between her and the interior,

and found the human dwelling to be impermeable.

The dog and the cat within glared at her,

but could do no more than bark and paw at the glass, harmlessly.

The human within did nothing but stare.

The bobcat mother acted as if she belonged.

As time passed, without more than a few harmless knocks,

she believed it, too.

Soon all were used to each other,

coexisting

throughout the stormy springtime nights,

as the bobcat's kits played merrily in the grass.

In time, the bobcats would leave

for a den in the hills, rich with prey,

but every so often,

one would shelter there,

next to the human, the dog, and the cat,

confident that they belonged.

Endnotes

1: Wolves in the wild do not actually have a strict Alpha-Beta-Omega conformation. The real hierarchies are much more nuanced, and the original researcher has actually published material that addresses this. However, several works of fiction, including realistic fiction, involving wolves has used this dynamic, and this poem attempts to use this dynamic to make a point – so please forgive the inaccuracy.

Author's Biography

Anna Schoenbach is a Freelance writer tapping away at her keys in the Washington, D.C. area. She writes science by day and fiction by night, and is published on the Coffin Bell website, in the OWS Primal Elements anthology, and frequently writes for health and medical blogs across the internet.

Anna tries to approach the human (and animal) elements of both wonder and horror, trying new directions even as she navigates the labyrinth of adulthood.

Her short stories can be found in the "Elements of Horror: Fire" anthology by Red Cape Publishing and "Monsters vs Nazis" by Deadman's Tome Press.

Artist Credits

Meg Houghton is an avid writer, board game enthusiast, and animal lover with both wildlife and chickens in her Everett, Washington backyard.

When she isn't taking care of her sweet, blind dog and her new garden, or participating in forum roleplay with friends online, she does digital illustration... sometimes. Other times, she cooks, cleans, and takes care of her household. She is a busy gal!

You can see her art (including the full-color illustrations featured in this book) at her Tumblr blog, here:

https://www.tumblr.com/blog/micillia